W9-BHG-200

ARTHUR HOWARD

Serious Trouble

VOYAGER BOOKS
HARCOURT, INC.
Orlando Austin New York San Diego Toronto London

Requests for permission to make copies of any part of the work should be submitted online at
www.harcourt.com/contact or mailed to the following address:
Permissions Department, Harcourt, Inc., 6277 Sea Harbor Drive, Orlando, Florida 32887-6777.

www.HarcourtBooks.com

First Voyager Books edition 2007

Voyager Books is a trademark of Harcourt, Inc.,
registered in the United States of America and/or other jurisdictions.

The Library of Congress has cataloged the hardcover edition as follows:
Howard, Arthur.
Serious trouble/Arthur Howard.
p.   cm.
Summary: Despite the objections of his very serious parents, Prince Ernest longs to become a jester,
and this helps him in an encounter with a three-headed dragon.
[1. Fairy tales.   2. Fools and jesters—Fiction.   3. Dragons—Fiction.]   I. Title.
PZ8.H83215Se   2003
[E]—dc21   2002014123
ISBN 978-0-15-202664-6
ISBN 978-0-15-205853-1 pb

A C E G H F D B

The display type was hand lettered by Arthur Howard.
The text type was set in Saint Albans.
Color separations by Bright Arts Ltd., Hong Kong
Printed and bound by Tien Wah Press, Singapore
Production supervision by Christine Witnik
Designed by Arthur Howard and Judythe Sieck

For Bill, Marjorie, Julie, Peter, Bon, Teddy, Linda, Jeremy, and Allyn

King Olaf and Queen Olive were serious people. They read serious books, they said serious things, and when they finally had a son, they named him the most serious name they could think of: Ernest.

"He'll be just like us," the king told the queen.

But the queen had serious doubts. "You'd better have a talk with him," she told her husband. "A serious talk."

So right after lunch, the king said,
"Son, one day you will be king, and being king
is no laughing matter."

"But I don't want to be king," said Ernest.

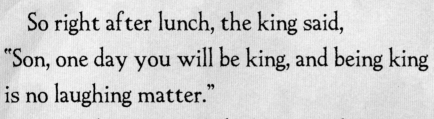

"Nonsense," replied His Royal Highness.
"Everyone wants to be king."

"Not me. I want to be a jester."

"A jester?"

"You know, someone who makes people laugh."

"This is no time to be funny!" roared His Majesty.
"We have a serious problem around here—a fire-breathing,
people-eating, three-headed DRAGON!"

A dragon was certainly nothing to laugh about.
Even Ernest knew that.

Still, he wanted to try being a jester at least once. So the next day he tiptoed past the royal guard…

…slid down the royal banister, and rushed outside. He had a couple of jokes he wanted to tell. All he needed was an audience.

As it turned out, he didn't have to look very hard, for suddenly…

…he was face-to-face-to-face-to-face with the fire-breathing, people-eating, three-headed DRAGON. Ernest was so scared, he couldn't say a word. The dragon, on the other hand, was surprisingly talkative.

"I'm Snaggle," said the head with the longest fangs.

"I'm Snuffle," said the head with the reddest snout.

"I'm Snide," said the head with the sharpest tongue.
"And I'm going to gobble you up."

"Please don't," begged Ernest.

"Oh yes, I will," said Snaggle.

"Oh no, you won't," said Snuffle.

"Maybe we will and maybe we won't," said Snide.

Like so many three-headed creatures, this dragon
could never make up its minds—it couldn't decide when
to go to bed, who to have for lunch, or even what to
call itself: Me, Us, or Hey You!

While the dragon bickered amongst itselves,
Ernest dashed away...

…but he didn't get far.

"Tell us a little about yourself," said Snide.
"I like to know who I'm eating."

"Well," said Ernest, "I'm...a jester."

"You? A jester?" said Snaggle. "Don't make me laugh."

"But I *can* make you laugh," said Ernest. "I really can."

"Impossible," said Snuffle. "We haven't laughed in a thousand years."

That gave Ernest an idea. "If I make you laugh, will you let me go?"

"He must be mad," said Snaggle.

"He might be tasty," said Snuffle.

"He could be funny," said Snide. "We'll give you two chances. Or maybe three."

So Ernest made a funny face.

"Not funny enough," snarled Snaggle.

"Not monstrous enough," snorted Snuffle.

"Quit while you've got a head," snapped Snide.

So Ernest tried a flip. But the flip was a flop.

"I'm getting a headache," said Snaggle.

"I'm getting bored," said Snuffle.

"I'm getting very, very hungry," said Snide.

Ernest had one chance left. But no matter how
hard he tried, he couldn't think of anything funny.
"I should have stayed home and just been a king,"
he said to himself.

The dragon, meanwhile, was getting impatient. It gnashed
its teeth. It blew smoke rings. It tapped its hairy toes.

Those toes gave Ernest another idea....

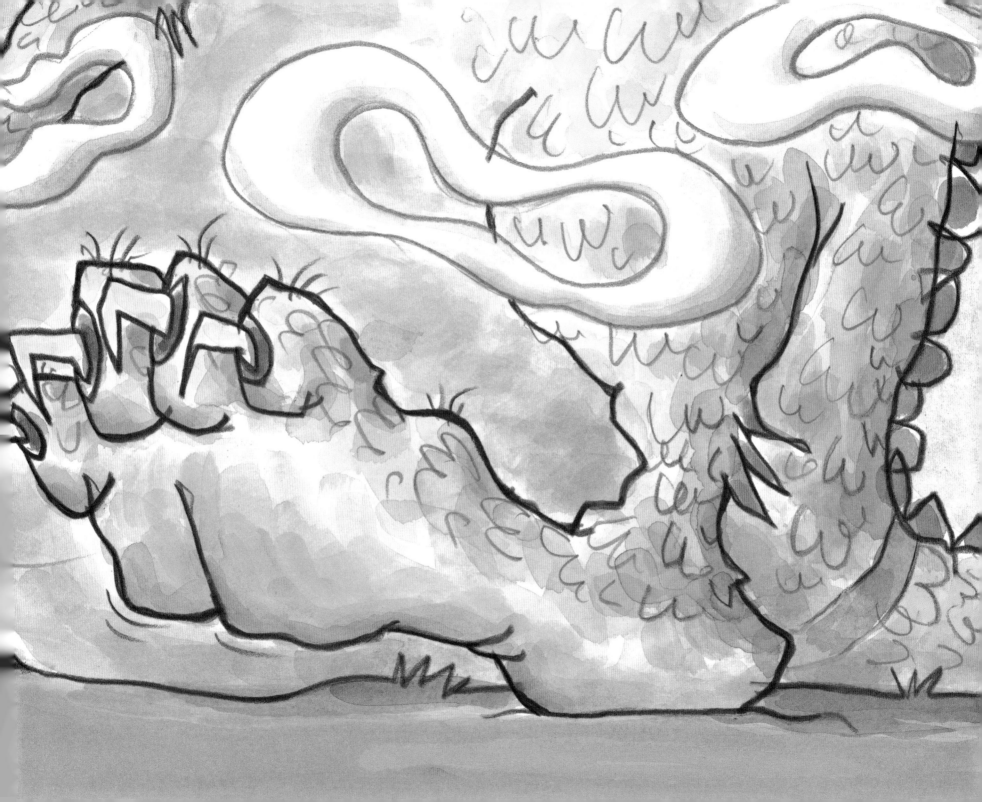

TICKLING!

And before you could say, "Snaggle, Snuffle, and Snide," that dragon was laughing so hard, huge tears poured down its snouts.

"Please. PLEASE. PLEASE!" it cried. "No more tickling!"

"Only if *you* stop gobbling people up," said Ernest.

To which the dragon said...

hat happened next? Some people say
Ernest ran all the way back to the castle and was never
funny again. He read serious books, said serious things,
and never, ever got into trouble.

But others insist the tale ends quite differently.
They say when Ernest got home, he told his parents
all about the dragon. As you can imagine,
Their Majesties were delighted.

...and it promised NOT to gobble up any more people!

"This calls for a celebration!" said the king.

So Ernest put on a show for them.
He flipped without flopping.

Knock, knock!

He joked without stopping.

He even juggled without dropping.
And for the grand finale …

…he shared the spotlight with a friend of his.

Which version of the story is true?
As the dragon might say, I'll give you two guesses…

...or maybe three.